Too Many Monsters

SUSAN MEDDAUGH

Houghton Mifflin Company Boston
1982

Library of Congress Cataloging in Publication Data
Meddaugh, Susan.
    Too many monsters.
    Summary: Howard lives in a dark forest with ninety-
nine other monsters who love to frighten him, until a
tree falls and the sunlight sends all the mean monsters
away.
    [1. Monsters—Fiction] I. Title.
PZ7.M51273Tn   [E]   81-7068
ISBN 0-395-31862-9   AACR2

For a family
of Finneys

In the deepest center
of the darkest forest
100 monsters lived.

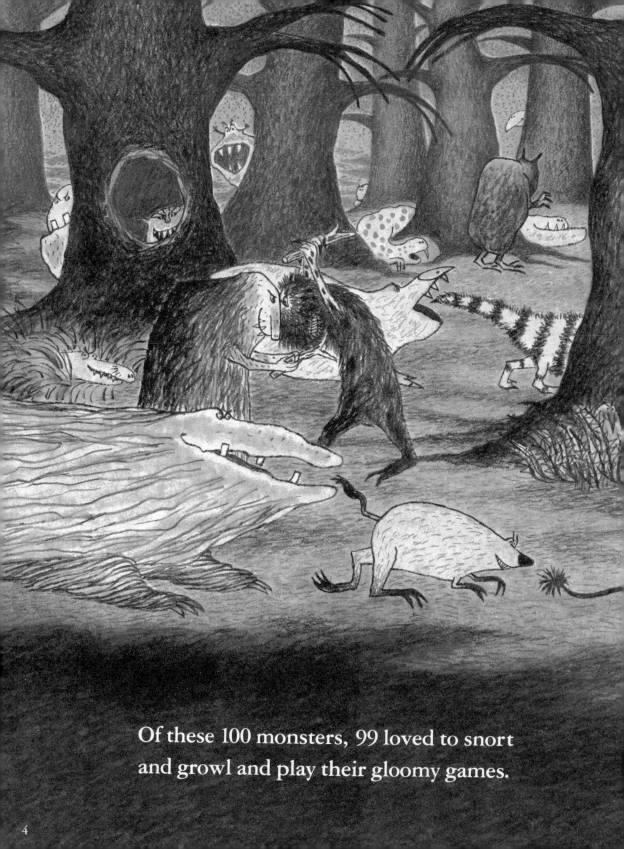

Of these 100 monsters, 99 loved to snort
and growl and play their gloomy games.

99 were happy to be mean.
Only one was not.

"It's always dark here," said Howard.

"And," he whispered, "There are
too many monsters."

99 monsters loved to frighten Howard.

"Leave me alone," he said.
But 99 monsters never gave Howard
one moment's peace.

"Being mean is fun," they laughed.
"I've got to find a nicer place to live,"
thought Howard.

So, Howard went looking for a new home.
He traveled east and west.
He went both north and south.

It was always the same.

It was dark.

And there were still too many monsters.

"The world is a scary place," he sighed.

Then a flash of bright color caught
his eye.

"What a beautiful little creature!"
said Howard.

"What a helpless little creature!"
growled 99 monsters.
They leaped and tumbled after it.
They tried to catch it in their wicked paws.

But the tiny creature flew up
and out of reach.
99 monsters were very unhappy.

Until they remembered Howard.

"Howard cannot fly," they said.

"Wait for me," cried Howard. "I'm
coming with you."

He started to climb the tree.

Howard pulled himself from branch
to branch.
The higher he climbed, the better he
liked it.

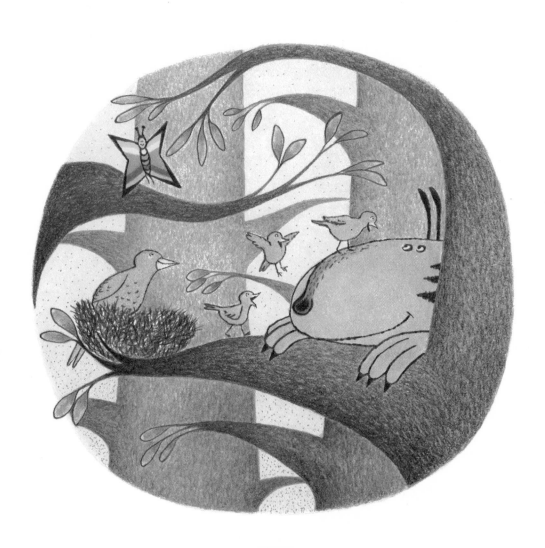

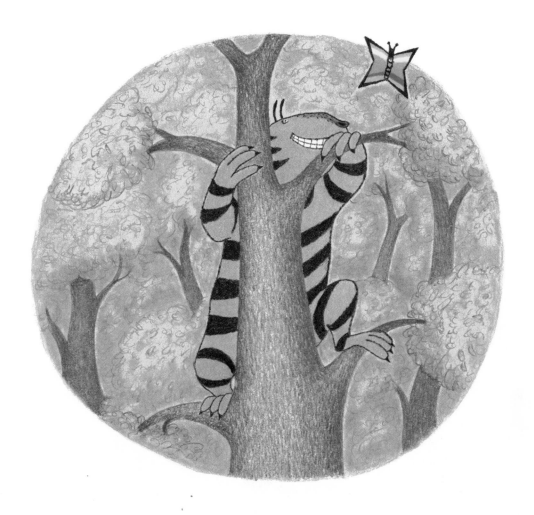

So, he climbed even higher, until
finally, he saw what no other monster
had ever seen.

Howard saw the sun.

But down below there were nasty smiles
on 99 awful faces.
"Howard is trapped in this tree," said
the monsters.

They started to climb up after him.
The tree began to bend.
It shook and swayed.

"Stop!" cried Howard.
But it was too late.
There were too many monsters for
one tree to hold.
The tree fell down to the ground.

99 monsters blinked
and squinted.
They howled in horror
as sunlight poured into
the forest.

"This is no place for monsters!" they cried, and they ran back into the dark.

Now, in the deepest center of the
darkest forest, 99 flowers bloom.

"It's not dark here," says Howard.
"It's not at all scary. And best of all,"
he says, "there are no monsters here."